Cats
and
Kites
and
Marmalade

Written and illustrated by

A.B.Wyze

ISBN 9798519001885

2021

Book
Three

CONTENTS

CATS AND DOGS

"That cats and dogs don't get along
has always been well known.
A dog would rather chase a cat
than chew a juicy bone.

But ask a dog why this is so,
he will not have a clue.
He'll say, "I just like chasing cats,
it's something all dogs do."

But cats all know why dogs give chase,
it's clear as clear could be.
The reason that they hate us so
comes down to jealousy.

For dogs they have to work so hard,
while cats have got things sussed.
A dog will even jump through hoops
to gain his master's trust.

A dog will go out on a lead,
in any weather, see.
A dog will chase a stick or ball
to show his loyalty.

And then of course he'll wag his tail,
pretending he is pleased.
He'll sit, he'll beg, lay down, play dead...
A cat does none of these.

For if a cat needs pampering,
a stroking of her fur.
She climbs upon her owner's knee
and simply has to purr.

A dog will guard a house at night,
another feline perk.
A cat will sleep that whole night through
while dogs do all the work.

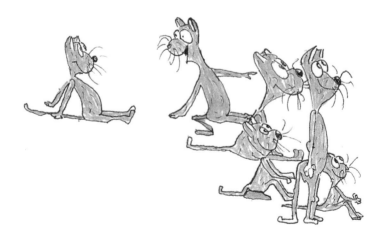

Why cats and dogs don't get along
is easy to explain.
When God created them you see,
us cats got all the brains."

I MET A CROCODILE

I met a Crocodile
as I walked down this lane.
His grin it seemed went round his head
and then came back again.

"Good morning sir," I gasped
and smiled a nervous smile.
"You teeth are quite the best I've seen
upon a Crocodile."

And THAT was a mistake.
I've never been so scared.
He grabbed me round the neck
and then he stared a hungry stare.

His teeth were needle sharp.
His mouth it opened wide.
"You seem to like my teeth," he smirked
"why don't you step inside?"

"Please sir do not eat me,"
my voice was very weak.
His claws pressed hard against my throat
so I could hardly speak.

My body turned to jelly.
My head it just went numb.
I couldn't feel my fingers
and I couldn't feel my thumbs.

"A CROCODILE would eat you
he said, "more soon than later,
"but I'm more civilized than
that for I'm an Alligator."

He set me on the ground.
I walked back down the lane.
I promised him I'd never make
the same mistake again.

So if you take that pathway
and meet this Alligator...
Do not call him a Crocodile...
he might just terminate ya!

PET TALK

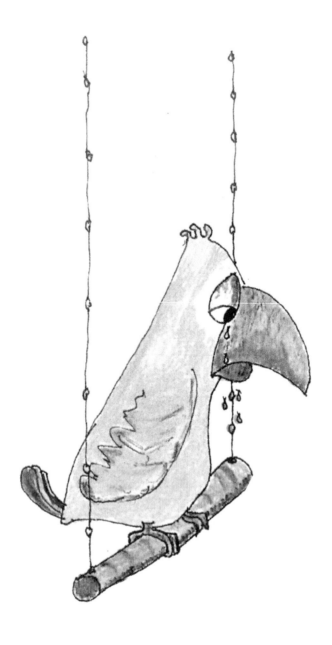

"Dogs can't talk no not a word
they'd rather chew a bone.
Cats can't talk but think they can,
and in that they're alone.

Fish can't talk their lips do move
but words just do not come.
Guinea Pigs, Chinchillas too
they both are just as dumb.

Tortoises can't talk at all
they're happy in their shell.
And hairy eight legged Spiders
they are all quite mute as well.

Rabbits? No they cannot talk
they'd rather chew a carrot.
So I'll just talk to my own self...
WE NEED ANOTHER PARROT!"

BUY ONE, GET ONE FREE

I walked past the Palais on Monday,
I don't go that way every day.
I stopped when I looked at the billboard,
and by gum it blew me away.

It said there in bold golden letters,
that glinted when they caught the light
that they had secured a late booking,
and Elvis were booked for the night.

Well I don't watch telly that often,
and I don't keep up with the news.
But I know it's been thirty years odd,
since Elvis has worn blue suede shoes.

I had twenty quid in me pocket,
and tickets cost eighteen it said.
I thought that's an absolute bargain,
to see someone sing who is dead.

The girl on the counter were foreign,
her accent were really quite strange.
I gave her the twenty for ticket.
She gave me a tenner in change.

Well I am a true northern person,
don't look a gift horse in the mouth.
And she were from somewhere unheard of,
she probably come from the south.

Well tickets sold out by the Sunday,
the queue were an absolute sight.
It went all the way back to Woolworths,
who'd stayed open late for the night.

Well I am a true northern person,
I can't pass a bargain up me.
I stared at a sign in their window,
it said buy one thing, get one free.

And I had ten quid in me pocket,
the show would not start until eight.
I said to the bloke stood behind me,
"can you save me place me old mate?"

Well he were a true northern person,
he said, "Aye I'll save it old lad.
But it's gonna cost you a quid like."
I said "righty ho that's not bad."

I took me nine quid into Woolworths,
I just did not have to think twice.
I mean, two for one is a bargain.
It makes every item half price.

But then I saw sign by the counter,
that dragged at me northerner's eyes.
It said if your spending a tenner,
you could win a fabulous prize.

The manager saw me gob open,
he came to stand right beside me.
He said in a really odd accent,
"It's buy one in here, get one free."

I pointed at sign by the counter,
me head it were in a right spin.
I said, "Is that right, spend a tenner,
and get a great prize if you win?"

He nodded and smiled... well me heart sank.
It sank to me shoes oh it did.
A chance in a northerner's lifetime,
and I only had the nine quid.

I took a quick glance out the window,
the queue it were passing straight by.
The manager looked out there with me.
I noticed a tear in his eye.

Now I am a true northern person,
and I spot a deal when it comes.
I took out me Elvis show ticket,
and said, "listen here me old chum."

Well he were a pushover really,
a southerner true through and through.
He fell for it hook line and sinker,
oh boy it was easy to do.

So I won the prize down at Woolworths,
a free DIY garden shed.
And he got to go and see Elvis.
They say that that man knocked em dead.

WHAT SHE WANTS

What she wants she said to me
it must impress her mates.
None of them she said to me
have personal licence plates.

What she wants I have to say
she usually gets.
She made her wishes public
and there's no-one taking bets.

I did try to change her mind
but she just called me tight.
So I searched the internet
through all the day and night.

Finally I found the plate
and boy it was not cheap.
Wrapped it up on Christmas Eve
and then went off to sleep.

Christmas came I took the gift
I handed it to her.
Ripping off the wrapping
oh, her hands were just a blur.

Well you should have seen her face
her jaw dropped to the floor.
Then she put her slippers on
and ran out of the door.

Forty seconds later and
she's back inside the room.
Giving me the blackest look,
a look that spells out doom.

I am just a simple man
well, that's what most men are.
I got her the licence plate...
and now she wants a CAR!

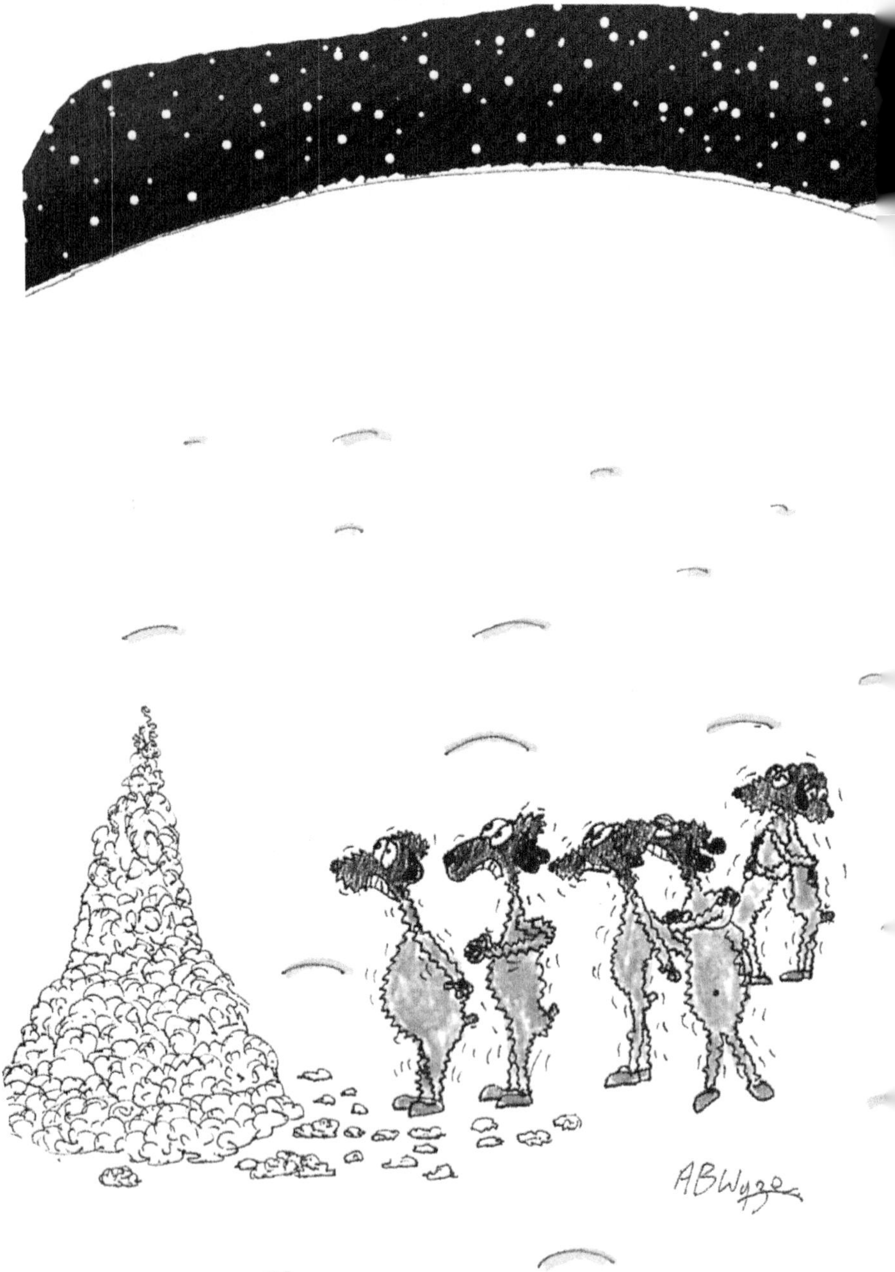
ABWyze

FARMER FRED'S SHEEP

You have to feel sorry
for Farmer Fred's sheep,
he took from them something
they wanted to keep.

The way they protested
would make your eyes weep.
But they could do nothing...
too tired...half-asleep.

And now their warm coats
are piled high in a heap.
More snow is predicted
some say, two feet deep.

You have to feel sorry
for Farmer Fred's sheep!

ONCE I CAUGHT A MEASLE

Oh, once I caught a measle...
not loads and loads, just one.
I stepped out of the shower
and saw it on me bum.

Well, my mate Mick had thousands
and stayed off school for weeks.
I got just one measle,
there on my right cheek.

I wrapped a towel round me
and ran to tell my Mum.
"Hey Mum I've caught a measle,
it's right here on me bum."

Now some words can be spoken
and some words you should think.
And 'bum' is just is just for thinking,
she kicked up such a stink.

It took at least an hour
for Mum's bad mood to cool.
She packed my lunch and satchel
and packed me off to school.

Well, my mate Mick walked with me
and he still had some spots.
I told him of me measle,
he said, "That's all you got?.

You can't get just one measle,
they don't go round in ones."
He pulled his shirt up, saying,
"I've still got bloomin' tons!"

When we got to our classroom
oh I was feeling bad
the measle on my bottom
was itching now like mad.

I squirmed around and wriggled,
I was in so much pain.
The teacher saw me squirming
and asked me to explain.

I told him of my measle,
my classmates they all laughed.
The teacher clipped my earhole
and told me I was daft.

He sent me to the matron
a right old battle axe.
She made me drop my trousers
and then said, "just relax…"

She said, "That's not a measle,"
and gave a sly old grin.
"It is a Mosquito bite,
I'll get the ointment tin."

Now when it comes to insects
there's nothing I don't know.
I pulled my pants up, shouting,
"Oh wow I've got to go."

And I ran so much faster
than I had ever run.
I sprinted through the school gates…
and home to tell me mum.

"Hey, Mum" I shouted loudly,
"I don't want this to scare ya,
but I've just seen the matron…
She says I've got malaria!"

WHITE OUT

I telephoned Miranda,
now she's a Scottish lass.
She said the weather there
is very bleak.
She said the snow's been falling
for nearly seven days.
They say," she said,
"it's set for one more week.

No-one's going anywhere
the snow is far too deep.
The schools are closed
the shops are out of bounds.
The temperature is frightening
it's now thirteen below.
I'm so surprised
the telephones aren't down.

My husband," said Miranda,
"stands there at the window.
in his hand he holds
a glass of gin.
He's been there for ages now,
it doesn't bother me...
I'll never let
the drunken blighter IN."

NEXT DOOR'S CAT

Next door's cat don't live next door
no, next door's cat lives here!
Sits upon our window sill
and grins from ear to ear.

I am not a fan of cats
but in that I'm alone.
I don't like its creepy smile
it chills me to the bone.

My wife loves that cat she does
adores that scary smile.
She goes shopping every day
straight down the pet food aisle.

Next door's cat don't eat at home
no, next door's cat eats here.
Lives on salmon vol au vents
and even drinks me beer.

I am not a fan of cats
as I've already said.
Words were said, quite angry words,
and now I'm in me shed.

Eat me meals down here I do
me wife were clear on that.
I asked her to choose you see
and she chose next door's cat.

Next door's cat sits on that sill
and grins down at me shed.
Next door's cat looks fit and well
and unlike me... well fed!

"Something must be done," I said,
"can't stand this anymore,"
I packed up my sleeping bag
and headed for next door.

Her next door is twice my size;
intimidating sort.
But I simply stood my ground
and told her what I thought.

"My wife's kicked me out!" I yelled,
"I'm sleeping in me shed.
Now your cat's in residence,
she's sharing my wife's bed!"

Well, she looked me up and down
then grinned from ear to ear
"Oh, I liked that cat I did,"
she whispered with a sneer.

"Then the cat from one door down
replaced her just like that.
And I'll say quite honestly
I love my next-door cat.

If you don't believe me lad,
my husbands here," she said.
"I'll unlock the gate for you...
he's sleeping in our shed!"

MURDER

I didn't mean to do it guv
it happened by mistake.
The evidence is piling up
oh give a guy a break.
They'll put me up before a judge
I'll end up doin' time.
How could I know that poetry
was never meant to rhyme?
I went and murdered poetry
I did it, it was me.
I went and used all rhyming words
how stupid could I be?
The poetry police have shown
my face to everyone.
I went and murdered poetry
and now I'm on the run.

OCTOBER

October, October
you got here at last
and now it's the end of the waiting.
I'm off down the High Street
I'm taking my bags
cos now I can start celebrating.
October I love you
I can't say how much
the summer was ever so boring.
The air was too hot
and the days were too long
my blood pressure
must have been soaring.
October, October
you're my favourite month
and now there will be
no more waiting.
The shops are all packed
with those Christmassy things
and now we can start celebrating!

THE INDIAN FORECAST

Oh, Walking Bear the Cheyenne chief
he had to play the part.
His tribe were all now asking him
when wintertime would start.

They needed some assurances
as skies were turning grey
and Walking Bear, their ageing chief,
was versed in olden ways.

They watched him through admiring eyes
and they were all so sure
that Walking Bear, the ancient one,
would know what was in store.

Though this was now the modern-day
of weather satellites
the braves still trusted Walking Bear
to get predictions right.

And Walking Bear he understood
he must not let them down
but secretly he had no clue...
so he went into town.

And in the town, the payphone stood
he squeezed himself inside.
He felt a little guilty though
it cannot be denied.

He phoned the weather centre up,
he needed answers fast...
He asked if this late summer warmth
was probable to last.

He rode back to his waiting tribe
as quickly as he could.
He said the winter might be bad
and they should fetch some wood.

For he recalled the mighty freeze
and storms of eighty-six.
When Indians were without fire
when they ran out of sticks.

The Indians all then dispersed
in groups of four and six.
They foraged and they searched around
for likely looking sticks.

They filled their bags with firewood
and brought it back to camp.
For Walking Bear had indicated
months of cold and damp.

So, Walking Bear went back to town
to use the phone again.
He asked the distant weatherman
"You're certain it will rain?

You're certain that the coming months
will not be very nice?
With wind and pouring rain and snow
and frozen lakes of ice?"

The weatherman said "certainly
our methods are unique.
And we can tell this winter will be
freezing, cold and bleak."

So Walking Bear he rode back home
to speak to all his braves.
"My bones say we must search again
for wood that we can save."

So far and wide they searched around
to gather what they could.
They filled the wigwams, filled the camp
with piles and piles of wood.

And Walking Bear rode into town
to use the phone again.
He asked how they could be so sure
about the snow and rain.

The weatherman replied with words
that shook him to the core.
"Oh, satellites are useful tools
but we have something more."

"We know the winter will be bad,
much worse than eighty-six
because the Indians near here
are stockpiling on sticks."

SPIDERS IN COLUMBIA

Don't go to Columbia
it's such a scary land.
Spiders in Columbia
grow bigger than your hand.

And they don't hide in corners,
they come out in plain sight.
Looking for someone like you
to give a nasty fright.

Though they may eat flies and stuff,
they have such fearsome jaws
the next leg they'll be biting
could very well be yours.

You're safer in your country
where spiders are so small.
Where spiders run away from you,
you won't be scared at all.

Though crows will eat a spider
here's something you should know....
Spiders in Columbia
will eat the blooming crow!

WHO YOU ARE

When I met May I said ok
my mission is complete.
I'll marry her
we'll have eight kids
and life will be complete.
Then May met Arthur Huddlestone
and I tasted defeat.
Cause his mum owned a sweet shop
on the corner of our street.
He wooed her with a barley cane
the dirty rotten cheat.

When I met Rose
I said God knows
where this affair will end.
The look she gave assured me
she was much more than a friend.
Then Rose met Barry Bannister
it drove me round the bend.
That Barry had a skipping rope
and he gave her a lend.
It took at least a fortnight for
my broken heart to mend.

When I met Sue
I'm telling you
my heart began to soar.
She knocked the socks off
all the girls
I'd ever known before.
Then Sue met Ernie Whistlethwaite
whose parents owned a store.
And he was ten
and I was eight
I never felt so sore.

Shirley, Brenda
Sally too,
I never took them out.
And all because
they looked at me
and saw that I have nowt.
And now I'm nine
and I have learned
and don't have any doubts.
It isn't who you are at all...
it's what you have that counts.

MISS NICEDAY

We've got a brand-new nanny.
Miss Niceday is her name.
I'm not sure that I like her.
My sisters feel the same.
Our parents they adore her.
They rave about her skills.
But we are closest to her.
She gives us all the chills.
And now she's cooking dinner.
Our parents are not here.
Oh man, she has us worried.
She's guzzled all the beer.
Today she taught us English.
All anagrams and stuff.
Now we have done some thinking.
And we have thought enough.
We're with her in the kitchen
and we've all had to hide.
An anagram of Niceday
comes out as cyanide!

KITES

While buying kites ain't difficult,
flying them's another.
So many holes, so many strings,
can't tell one from t'other.

It takes two hours but finally
my kite is all prepared.
So off I go down to the beach
to get it in the air.

But as I run along the beach
the string held in my hand,
the wind is like a Hurricane,
the kite drags in the sand.

Those tiny mites are flying kites
and granddads from deck chairs.
I even saw a labrador
its kite high in the air.

Buying kites ain't difficult
but flying them who cares?
I think I'll hire a deck chair
and watch them all fly theirs.

THE DAY THE EARTH...

The undertaker undertook
a task of magnitude.
The astrophysics lecturer
did something slightly rude.

A door-to-door Jehova's Witness
set himself a goal.
A farmer stood and stared
into a dirty great big hole.

And all this time the anchor man
was wishing he was ill.
Upon the day the aliens
made all the world stand still.

A prisoner was checking out
his super stripy tan.
An Eskimo was tucking
into tuna from a can.

A lawyer and his lover
were comparing alibis.
A sailor lost at sea
was staring blankly at the skies.

A diner was deliberating,
checking out his bill.
Upon the day the aliens
made all the world stand still.

A crooked cop was counting out
his counterfeit reward.
A movie star was cleaning
her academy award.

A bell boy smoked a cigarette
behind the blue hotel.
A sinner was repenting
lest he end his life in Hell.

A senator was pressing through
an immigration bill.
Upon the day the aliens
made everything stand still.

A doctor told a patient
not to plan too far ahead.
A sixty-year-old groupie
dragged a drunken star to bed.

A schizophrenic priest
was all alone attending Mass.
A prince stood on a staircase
with a slipper made of glass.

An alcoholic told his wife
that she looked really ill.
Then of course those aliens
made everything stand still.

A midwife held a baby up
and smacked its bottom hard.
A husband lost his home
upon the turn of just one card.

A clown sat by the fireside
and watched the wax paint run.
A soldier in the front line
fixed a bayonet to his gun.

And butterflies like frozen flags
were static on the hill.
Upon the day the aliens
made all of us stand still.

The aliens walked on the earth
to see what they had done.
Their shadows skipped and shimmied
from the brightness of our sun.

SARA COURT

Oh, spare a thought for Sara Court
it did not go as planned.
She built herself an aeroplane
from what she had at hand.

Some aluminium dustbin lids,
a cylinder or two.
Some metal strips and bulldog clips
and several tubes of glue.

Some brackets, bolts, some sheets of tin
whatever could be found.
And then she tied on fireworks
to get it off the ground.

Oh, spare a thought for Sara Court
she did not get it right.
She pulled her plane up to the cliffs
to do her maiden flight.

They counted down from ten to one,
the ambulance stood by.
And then they lit the fireworks...
she launched into the sky.

Oh, spare a thought for Sara Court
she found out way too late
that all those tubes of superglue
were past their use-by date.

Oh, Sara flew that aeroplane
so very, very high.
Then bits of this and bits of that
just fell out of the sky.

Oh, spare a thought for Sara Court
and then spare just one more.
She'd made herself a parachute
from her mum's knicker drawer.

Her mother's bulging bloomers
they ballooned above her head.
The legs had holes, the air rushed through,
so to the ground she sped.

They found her plane a mile away
all piled up on the heath.
Oh, spare a thought for Sara Court,
they found her underneath.

Now, hold that thought for Sara Court
despite her hurt and pain
she hobbled home her head held high
to build another plane!

DREAMS

When you go to bed
and lay down your head
be sure to
remember your name.
Or you may soon dream
the wrong person's dream,
and that's just not
playing the game.
Besides, if you do,
all hell could ensue
you'll open
all kinds of locked doors.
For all dreams you know
need somewhere to go,
and somebody else may dream yours.

HANDS IN POCKETS

Hands in pockets
no direction
only standing
for election.
Open boxes
check for crosses
soon they'll know
just who the boss is.
Wear that rosette
on your jacket
soon you'll surely
earn a packet.
Hands in pockets
no direction
only standing
for election.

MERRIE CHRISTMAS

Oh, Robin Hood sat in a tree
he'd been up there since six
and Christmas day was coming fast
the man was in a fix.

Yes, this was something new to him
and he felt so unsure.
He had not had a sweetheart
to buy presents for before.

Though Marion insisted that
his love was gift enough
he knew that if he gave her nought
she'd make his life so tough.

But Robin Hood he had no cash
he'd given it away.
The poor were buying gifts
for all their friends on Christmas day.

Then Little John decided
that his leader needed aid.
He called the gang together
and they went out on a raid.

Of course they got some bounty
yes, some gold and so much more.
Of course they did the right thing...
and they gave it to the poor.

But they kept back one item
oh, it really was quite good.
They wrapped it up and gave it
to a thankful Robin Hood.

He wrote a loving label
and he stuck some holly on.
He thanked his merrie outlaws...
gave a hug to Little John.

He rode up to the castle
and he wore a thick disguise.
He found his true love's chamber
and left his sweet surprise.

And then on Christmas morning
he was waiting by the tree
for Marion his darling
to reward him lovingly.

He saw her horse approaching
and he waved without a sound.
She galloped over to him...
and she knocked him to the ground.

"You imbecile," she shouted,
"Oh, I have no words to speak.
That trinket that you gave me...
it was thieved from me last week!"

DEBRA THE ZONKEY

Debra the zonkey now she is a cross...
a very cross, cross she is too.
Mum was a donkey, dad was a zebra
they met quite by chance in the zoo.

Some silly keeper left a gate open
and dad thought that mum looked quite hot.
Soon as he saw her; he was enamoured
he just had to give it a shot.

Debra the Zonkey has her own paddock
she does not have one single mate..
That's why she's angry, feeling so bitter,
it's all down to one unlocked gate.

NEVER TRUST A LOBSTER

NEVER TRUST A LOBSTER

I met a lobster in the lobby
looking for a bed.
He said, "I'll pay good money,
I am good for it," he said.
I said, "I have the perfect place
for you to rest your head."

Then as I ran the bath tap
oh he listened to it glug.
He looked at me suspiciously
and said, "I'm not a mug.
You'll take my money, put me in
and then you'll pull the plug."

I promised him quite faithfully,
"I'm not that kind of chap."
Persuaded him convincingly,
"It's not some kind of trap."
He wrote a cheque and climbed right in,
and turned on both the taps.

From Thursday through to Monday
he just soaked the days away.
I fed him fresh grilled salmon cakes
upon a silver tray.
On Monday afternoon, he left,
and thanked me for the stay.

He asked to use the telephone
to telephone a cab.
He said he'd pay me later...
I should 'put it on the tab.'
The taxi drove up instantly
well driven by a crab.

The crafty old crustacean
he climbed straight into his seat.
It took a while because you know
a lobster has ten feet.
He tossed me 20p and said
that I was 'rather sweet.'

The postman called next morning,
right on time as you'd expect.
On opening the letter oh,
I felt a total wreck.
The lobster's bank regretfully
had bounced the lobster's cheque.

So never trust a lobster
never shake one by the claw.
A lobster will take anyone
for everything I'm sure.
Be wary if a lobster
should come knocking on your door.

But if a lobster calls on you
I honestly suggest
you pop him in a bath tub
and then boil the thieving pest.
Then toss him in a salad
as a starter for your guests.

WE LIKE IT HERE

Said squirrel red to squirrel grey,
"What brings you round about this way?"
Said squirrel grey to squirrel red,
"I'm lost, I'm tired I need a bed."

Said squirrel red to squirrel grey,
"Come home with me, I'll let you stay."
So squirrel red took squirrel grey
to share his warm and cosy drey.

The hours turned into a day.
"I like it here," said squirrel grey.
"I have some friends who'd like it too,
pray, can they come and stay with you?"

"Of course they can," said squirrel red,
"as long as they supply a bed."
And so it was that squirrel grey,
departed from that cosy drey.

The hours turned into a day
and squirrel red missed squirrel grey.
But busy was his middle name,
and finding acorns was his game.

He foraged through the woodland floor
and filled his secret acorn store.
The days they passed and turned to weeks.
He filled his store...He filled his cheeks.

Then on one cold late autumn day
he saw a squirrel, it was grey.
Not one, but two, not two, but four,
not four but eight, and many more.

The trees turned grey with squirrel fur.
The woodland floor was one grey blur.
They scurried round, and what was more,
they found the secret acorn store.

"They like it here," said squirrel grey,
"please tell me friend you'll let them stay."
"Of course they can," said squirrel red.
"We like it here," the grey ones said.

The weeks sped by and turned to years,
said squirrel grey, "We like it here."
He went to look for squirrel red,
and found him packing up his bed.

"I'm going north," said squirrel red,
"why don't you come along?" he said.
"No thank you friend," said squirrel grey,
"We like it here, I think we'll stay."

Said squirrel grey to squirrel red,
"You'll have a long, long road ahead."
Said squirrel red to squirrel grey,
"The stars will guide me on my way."

It's cold the further north you go,
the rain turned slowly into snow.
But squirrel red was squirrel bold.
He just marched on, ignored the cold.

Two long weeks passed, then five, then ten.
He found a wooded Scottish glen.
The trees were sturdy, tall and strong.
He said "This is where I belong."

He heard a noise, he turned his head.
He saw a squirrel...It was red.
Not one but two, not two, but four.
Not four, not eight but many more.

"I'm home at last," said squirrel red
"I'll build a drey, I'll make a bed."
He whispered softly in his drey.
"I like it here...I think I'll stay."

CLASS SIZES

A Tiger
doesn't go to school.
A Cobra
does not go to school.
A Grizzly Bear
has never been to school.

And now I think I've worked it out.
And I am right, I have no doubt.
Though you might think
that I am just a fool.
It's why
there are so many kids at school.

Tarantulas
don't go to school.
Vampire Bats
don't go to school
A Scorpion
has never been to school.

It's obvious I have to say
why kids are piling up each day.
These creatures have been
banned by some old rule.
It's why
there are so many kids at school.

Anacondas?
None at school.
Great White
don't go to school
Jellyfish
with stings don't go to school.

But if they did I have to say
Results would be as plain as day
And though
you might call me a stupid fool
There would not be
so many kids in school

DOCTORS

Doctor Seuss, Doc Holiday
and Doctor Frankenstein,
sat around the mini bar
partaking of the wine.

Doctor Seuss picked up his pad,
he scribbled as he sipped.
"You creatin' stuff again?"
Doc Frankenstein then quipped.

"Every moment, every day,"
said good old Doctor Seuss.
"Waste of time," said Holiday,
"for we've all cooked our goose."

"Always kids who need a smile,"
old Doctor Seuss replied.
" I should not have to stop it now
... just because I died."

Frankenstein applauded,
then he drained his glass in one.
"Only YOU Doc, only you,
could sit HERE having fun."

Holiday stood to his feet
and pulled his Buntline out.
"Bring on all those Clanton boys,
you'll see what fun's about."

Frankenstein, he gave a grin
and poured another shot.
"They went to that other place,
where it's all nice and hot."

Doctor Seuss, he scribbled some
then ordered up a beer.
"Yes," he said, to Frankenstein,
"so how come YOU got here?"

Frankenstein sat on his stool
and drained his wine glass dry.
"Halloween, THAT saved me friend,"
he muttered with a sigh.

"All those kids that you wrote for,
well one night of the year,
they get loads of kicks they do,
by living close to fear."

God he works in strange old ways,
oh that I DO expect.
All those children have such fun,
He's just showed me respect."

Then a dwarf walked through the door,
just coming for some booze.
Followed by a shoemaker
in very trendy shoes.

"Howdy Doc," said Doctor Seuss,
"say what's your poison friend?"
"Apple juice," the dwarf replied,
"the good old Snow-White blend."

Then Doc Marten, parked his butt
and gave the air a sniff.
"Something smells," he softly said,
"oh what's that awful whiff?"

"It is YOU," said Holiday,
he lit up a cheroot.
"When's the last time Doc my friend,
that you changed your old boots?"

Marten gave a sly old grin
as he took to his stool.
"Show me ONE who don't wear these,
and I'll show YOU a fool."

"Doc is right," said Doctor Seuss,
"and I can second that."
Then he showed a drawing
of a cat in boots and hat.

All the doctors in the world
please read this piece and learn.
You could all be in this room
when it comes to your turn.

There's a place for all of us
and you'll be here, you'll see.
Telling tales and drinking wine
throughout eternity.

A MEMORABLE DAY OUT

"Oh, please it can't be wet.
Oh, please let it be dry."
I pull the curtains wide,
there's no cloud in the sky.

Daddy dresses granddad
while mummy toasts some bread.
Gives a slice to granddad,
he puts it on his head.

We all get in the car
a Micra's far too small,
and even sitting down
my Granddad's still quite tall.

"So what's the time?" he asks,
"and where's the Buffet Car?
Who has all our tickets?
It's much too cramped by far."

A mystery trip said Dad...
no mystery to me.
We've done this twice before...
we're going to the sea!

I like the zoo, it's cool
it's wicked is the zoo,
then granddad gives that look
that says he likes it too.

I asked him with a smile
if he'd been here before.
He said he wasn't certain
but now he's not so sure.

Parrots keep us talking
hyenas make us laugh.
Granddad makes a Monkey face
I take his photograph.

We see some wicked wolves
some humpy Camels too.
Granddad has an accident
just outside the loo.

Micras are quite tiny
you'd never give a lift,
when you have four people
and a zillion gifts.

I say to my Granddad,
"I loved that day with you."
He gives that certain smile
that only Granddads do.

He says "There's one more place
I'd like to take you to.
You will really love it...
I'll take you to the ZOO."

HUMPTY DUMPTY......THE TRUTH

Old Humpty Dumpty
he sat on the ground
feeling quite pleased
with the place he had found.
All the Kings horses
and all the Kings men
came from the inn
at a quarter-past-ten.
All of them drunk
from a party of fun.
Humpty was shattered
in more ways than one.
All the Kings men, yes,
and all the Kings steeds
thought for a minute
and quickly agreed.
Back to the palace
they went one and all
telling how how Humpty
had had a great fall.
"All of us tried,"
said the horses and men
"but none could put Humpty
together again."

WHO'S AFRAID.OF.MARMALADE?

I was afraid of marmalade
I never did know why.
I could not bear to have it near
no matter how I'd try.

An orange didn't bother me
and jam I just adore
but just a glimpse of marmalade
would chill me to the core.

I went to join the Navy
just to get away you see.
They said I'd need to be so brave,
I said, "there's nowt scares me."

But when I sat for breakfast
and the purser passed the toast,
all spread across that butter
was the thing I feared the most.

I ran out of the cabin
and I jumped into the sea
The shark infested ocean
it held little fear for me.

I wrestled with a giant crab
then climbed onto its back.
It took me to an island
where I came under attack.

Yes, seven giant spiders
all with countless staring eyes.
I wrenched a claw from Mr crab
and cut them down to size.

I ran into a nearby cave
and I could barely see.
Some vampire bats flew round my head
they didn't frighten me.

I climbed a spiral staircase
oh, it took a day or three.
I reached the highest place on earth,
but was I scared?...Not me.

I just removed my jacket
took my laces from my boots,
and well inside a minute
I had made a parachute.

A Pterodactyl then appeared,
it flew out of a cloud.
Its beak was wide its teeth were sharp
I merely laughed out loud.

I just took off my leather belt,
my trousers they fell down.
I lassoed Mr Dinosaur
and rode him to the ground.

And by the time we reached the ground
the dinosaur was tame.
"I'll keep you as a pet," I said;
"but first you'll need a name...

Now, Terry is too obvious
and Dino just won't do,
but Roger is a lovely name
so that's what I'll call you."

Well Roger gave a silly smile
and lifted up a leg.
And then I got the biggest shock
as Roger laid an egg.

"Well I can't call you Roger now,"
I started to explain.
"I know, I'll call you Florence,
as it was my mother's name."

The desert where we'd landed
was much hotter than it looked.
We had to find some shade
before the new-laid egg got cooked.

We found a cool dark cavern
where those scorpions all hide.
I picked them up and threw them out
and Florence stepped inside.

The egg began to crack and soon
young Roger's head appeared.
It had to be a boy of course,
cos girls do not have beards.

We fed him on some desert ants,
I caught some rattlesnakes.
We cooked them on an open fire
and cut them into steaks.

Then Florence caused the biggest shock
since Roger's egg was laid.
She pulled from underneath her wings
a jar of marmalade.

My body froze, my mouth went dry
my legs began to shake.
As Florence took the marmalade
and spread it on the steaks.

And then as quick as lightning,
as I broke into a sob
she grabbed a sticky snake steak
and she shoved it in my gob.

My head was filled with fireworks
my taste buds all went mad.
It was the most delicious grub
that I had ever had.

We waited till the night fell
and then Florence flew us home.
She flew us over Istanbul
she flew us over Rome.

I built a massive aviary
for her and Rog to share.
And now when I come home from work
I see smoke in the air.

We don't have any rattlesnakes
but earthworms by the ton.
They're lovely on the barbecue
if slightly underdone.

We cover them with marmalade
and share a flask of wine.
Young Roger has to use a straw
but Florence drinks just fine.

And now that orange marmalade
it holds no fears for me
I eat it for my breakfast
for my dinner and my tea.

I'm not afraid of marmalade
but do know some who are...
Those wriggly worms
all freeze with fear...

if they see just one jar.

WHEN

When cats have feathers, birds have paws,
snakes have feet and fish have claws.
When water only flows uphill
and ten add twenty comes to nil.
When yesterday has never been
and Mrs Spratt eats only lean.
When elephants start laying eggs
and centipedes have just two legs.
And when the sun stays out all night
and falling snow is black not white.
When camels walk across the sea
and breakfast comes just after tea.
And when spaghetti grows on trees
and pepper doesn't make you sneeze.
And when the earth goes round the moon
and Christmas day appears in June.
When rainfall is no longer wet...
I think my teacher MIGHT... forget.

THE END.

Other Books in This Series

1. Just Because You Are Growing Old it Does Not Mean That You Have to Grow Up.
2. Why Should Kids Get All the Fun Poems?

Other Books by A B Wyze

1. Back in the Days of Tanners and Bobs
2. Grannies and Granddads and Other Odd Folk
3. Air Dairve's Fust Booker Pomes
4. Giggle as You Go (Limericks for the Smallest Room)
5. Our Mavis

All books are available on Amazon and direct from the author.

contact:

abwyzestories@gmail.com

Printed in Great Britain
by Amazon

64127380R00047